# Kakah and the Priceless Treasure

By Priscila G. Alves
Illustrations by Natalia Soares

*Kakah And The*
*Priceless Treasure*
by Priscila G. Alves

Printed in the United States of America

ISBN 9781498477468



www.xulonpress.com

Kakah woke up and looked through
her window. It was a beautiful day in
the small town. It was the first day of
spring vacation.

The kids were very happy playing outside.

Jimmy and Lino chose to play soccer with
the new ball Jimmy got for Christmas.

Molly went for a bike ride.

Becca was at the little park playing on the swing once again!

Oh, it was a long winter and everyone was
very excited to be able to play outside.

Lolita, one of Kakah's best friends, did not go out to play. Kakah noticed that the window in her bedroom was still closed and wondered if Lolita was sick.

She decided to go and see if everything was ok . When she got to Lolita's house , she asked her mom if Lolita wanted to go out to play .

But to her surprise Lolita's mom said that it would not be possible. "Maybe next time," she replied.

Kakah was not very satisfied with the response. She wanted to know how to help her friend. Was Lolita sick? Or grounded? Hmmm...

It was such a long-awaited day for all the children on the street that she could not imagine seeing one of her beloved friends not enjoying it.

She decided to ask Lino, Lolita's brother, what had happened to Lolita.

Lino told her that Lolita didn't want to go out to play because her parents didn't buy her the scooter she wanted for her birthday.

She was very sad that everyone had new
toys and she didn't.

Lino also told her that his father couldn't buy a scooter because he had just lost his job.

As soon as Kakah heard the whole story
she decided to do something very special.

She asked Jimmy, Lino, Becca, and Molly
to bring outside the oldest toy they had.
It didn't matter if it was a ripped ball, or
a dirty doll...

"Please bring out your old toys and we'll
play with them after lunch!" she said.

While the kids went inside to find old toys,
she went home to open a special treasure
box Grandma had given her last year.

Looking at the special box, Kakah wrote
a beautiful letter to her friend Lolita.

"Dear Lolita, we missed you very much this morning. We all love to play with you, no matter which game is it! We don't care if your clothes are new, or your shoes have brand names on them, or even whether you've been on a cool vacation trip or not!"

Dear

"Last year when Daddy couldn't buy me a new bike, Grandma told me all about the priceless treasure!"

2

“She told me that I should be happy and enjoy every moment of my life with what I already have. It is really nice to get new toys or clothes, but the secret to being happy is to be thankful.”

“She also gave me this treasure box to always remind me what she said. We really love you and care about you!”

“After lunch we’ll all be playing with old toys outside. Would you like to join us? Love, Kakah and your friends!”

To: Lolita

"She went and knocked on Lolita's
window and dropped off the letter with
the treasure box for her .

As soon as she finished her lunch, Kakah went running outside to see if her plan had worked.

When she opened the door, she saw Lolita smiling
and playing with Molly with their old dolls.

Lolita loved the letter and understood that when we're thankful for what we have it's easier to have fun.

That was the first of many happy days in the small town!

Parents, grandparents, kids, pets . . . everyone together celebrating being thankful for what they had.

CPSIA information can be obtained
at www.ICGtesting.com
Printed in the USA
FSOW03n0325190716
22761FS